TO _____

DISNEY'S
SMALL WORLD LIBRARY
THE RUNAWAY KITE
An Adventure in Japan

GROLIER ENTERPRISES INC.
DANBURY, CONNECTICUT

Developed by The Walt Disney Company in conjunction with Nancy Hall, Inc.
ISBN 0-7172-8209-0

Mickey Mouse and Goofy gazed out the window of the bullet train, the fast-moving Japanese express train. They were on their way to Tokyo to see new and different things—and to make new friends.

As the train sped along, Mickey pointed out the sights. "Look, Goofy—there's Mount Fuji," he said. "It's the highest mountain in Japan."

"Where?" asked Goofy, scratching his head. "This train is moving so fast, I can hardly see a thing!"

"I guess the guidebook isn't kidding when it says this is one of the world's fastest trains," Mickey said with a laugh. "In fact, we're going to be in Tokyo very soon."

Sure enough, the bullet train began to slow down as it pulled into the station.

"Where should we begin?" asked Mickey as he and Goofy left the train station.

"With lunch!" Goofy answered happily. "Lunch is always a good place to begin!"

So the two friends walked down several blocks, and at last they came to what looked like a nice restaurant.

As they stood in the doorway Goofy whispered, "Are you sure this is a restaurant, Mickey? There aren't any chairs, and I don't see any silverware on the tables."

A moment later a woman in a kimono showed them to their seats, which were soft cushions on the floor.

"Gawrsh, things sure are different here," Goofy said cheerfully as he sat down.

The woman brought fish and rice for the two friends
to eat. She brought chopsticks, too, which the Japanese
use instead of forks.

Goofy couldn't pick up his fish with the chopsticks.
Mickey couldn't eat his rice.

"A guy could get really hungry here," said Goofy.

The woman in the kimono smiled. She showed
them how to hold the chopsticks, and at last they were
able to eat.

After lunch, Mickey and Goofy went to the Toy
Museum. It was filled with samples of kites for Boys' Day,
dolls for Girls' Day, games, and toy trucks and planes.
     They went to Edo Palace, where crowds of boys and
girls were lined up to have their pictures taken.

Boys were flying kites in the park near the palace. Mickey and Goofy saw big kites and small ones. They saw hawk kites and dragon kites. There was a kite that looked just like the palace. And they saw a kite that looked like something they had never seen before.

"What a great kite!" said Goofy.

The boy with the box kite grinned. "Tomorrow I will enter this in the kite contest," he said.

"A contest?" echoed Mickey. "Someone is having a kite contest?"

At that, three or four boys crowded close.

"It is for Boys' Day," said one of them.

"See the carp streamers on those houses?" asked another. "Those are for Boys' Day, too."

"On Boys' Day, there is a carp on every house for each boy that lives there," said a third boy. "The carp is our symbol for strength, and every Japanese boy hopes he will grow up to be strong and brave—like the carp!" he added proudly.

Then the boys raced away to fly their kites. Mickey and Goofy went on to the zoo. On the way they saw more boys. They saw more kites. They saw more carp streamers on the houses, too.

At the zoo, there were more boys flying kites. Goofy and Mickey saw butterfly kites. They saw a kite that looked like a big bee. They even saw a kite that looked like a caterpillar with a hundred legs.

"That kite contest must be a really big deal," Goofy said. "Looks like every kid in town will be in it. Do you think we could fly a kite in the contest, too, Mickey?" he asked hopefully.

"I don't think so, Goofy," Mickey replied. "It says in the guidebook that Boys' Day is only for boys."

"Okay, so we won't be in the contest," Goofy said. "But let's go get a kite and fly it anyway!"

"Good idea!" Mickey agreed. They hurried to a toy store, but they were too late. The man who owned the store had sold his last kite just that morning.

By now, Goofy had his heart set on flying a kite.

"I know," said Mickey, "let's make one that looks just like the box kite the boy we met earlier was flying. It will fly as well as anything we could buy."

So Goofy and Mickey found a store where a
shopkeeper sold them paper, bamboo sticks, glue, and
string. They bought everything they needed to make a
box kite.

"Where shall we go to make our kite, Goofy?" asked Mickey.

"How about the park over there?" Goofy replied.

"Good idea," said Mickey. "Come on."

They walked over to a quiet part of the park. They sat down and began to work on their kite. As they worked, bamboo sticks, paper, and string began to pile up around them. Perhaps it was not so easy to make a kite!

Just then a friendly police officer walked by. "What's the matter?" he asked.

"We're having trouble making a kite," said Mickey.
The policeman showed them how to tie the bamboo
sticks together and to glue on the paper.

Then the policeman showed them how to write the Japanese symbols for "good luck" and "happiness" to decorate their kite.

Mickey and Goofy thanked the policeman for his help. At last, their kite was ready to fly!

Goofy held the kite string and ran. The wind caught the kite, and it lifted way up into the sky.

"Yippeeeee!" cried Mickey.

Goofy ran faster and faster, gazing up at the kite as it blew across the sky. But he wasn't watching where he was going, and—CRASH—he tripped and fell flat on the ground.

"Ooof!" he groaned, letting go of the kite string.
"Oh, no!" cried Mickey.
The wind whirled the kite away above the rooftops.
"Stop!" shouted Mickey.
"Come back!" called Goofy.

Mickey and Goofy chased after the kite, running as fast as they could. They raced through the crowds that filled the busy streets. The two friends ran across bridges and rushed through parks and past people, never losing sight of their kite for a moment.

Suddenly the wind changed. The kite began to fall, plummeting through the sky until it disappeared behind a wall.

Mickey and Goofy stopped running and looked around. They were not on a busy street now. They were in a quiet lane. Before them they saw a wall, and through the gate they saw where the kite had fallen. Goofy peered through the gate and saw a tiny house with a carp streamer flying from the roof.

Goofy also saw a little boy talking excitedly to his mother. The boy was holding Goofy and Mickey's kite.

"Look!" said the boy. "It dropped from the sky."

"Kites do not just drop from the sky, Kenji," said his mother. "It must belong to someone."

At that, Goofy knocked a quick little knock on the gate.

Kenji turned to look at him. "Oh," he said. "This is your kite, isn't it?"

"Yep," replied Goofy. "My friend Mickey and I made it, but it ran away."

The boy looked sad as he handed back the kite. "If it were my kite, I could enter the contest tomorrow," said the boy slowly.

"Don't you have a kite of your own?" Mickey asked.

The boy did not. "I waited too long," he said. "When I went to the toy shop, all the kites were gone. I made one, but it wouldn't fly."

"Gawrsh!" said Goofy. Then he thought for a minute. "Our kite can fly. And we really wanted to enter it in the contest."

"But we can't be in the contest . . ." Mickey began.

"Unless we find a boy who can fly our kite," Goofy added. "Want to be our partner, Kenji?" he asked the boy.

"You can fly the kite," said Mickey. "Goofy and I will cheer!"

"You mean it?" asked Kenji joyfully. He was all smiles.

"We mean it," said the two friends.

So the next day Kenji flew the kite. Mickey and Goofy cheered.

Perhaps theirs might not have been the most beautiful kite in the contest. It might not have been the biggest. But Mickey and Goofy didn't care. They knew their kite was a wonderful kite, because it had helped them make a new friend in a faraway place.

Did You Know...?

Every country has many different customs and places that make it special. Some of the things that make Japan special are mentioned below. Do you recognize any of them from the story?

The Tokyo-Fukuoka express train, also called the bullet train, is one of the world's fastest passenger trains. It speeds between Tokyo, the capital of Japan, and the city of Osaka at 130 miles per hour.

Mount Fuji is the highest mountain peak in all of Japan. It is really a volcano, but it hasn't erupted in almost three hundred years, and the Japanese hope it never will again.

The Imperial Palace has been the official home of Japan's emperors for over one hundred twenty years. The palace is really a fort with bridges and moats.

Boys' Day in Japan is on May 5. For each son in a household, a carp streamer is flown from the roof of the house. On Boys' Day, boys fly kites and display dolls of great warriors and heroes.

Japanese girls have their own day, too. On Girls' Day, March 3, girls invite friends to see their beautifully dressed dolls and eat special rice cakes called *hisimochi*.

Japanese people eat with two sticks, known as chopsticks, instead of with forks. Mickey has gotten very good at eating *sushi*, raw fish wrapped around rice balls, with his chopsticks. Goofy prefers a hot drink of *miso* soup, which is made of seaweed and soybean paste.

A *kimono* is a robe made of silk or cotton. It has long, square sleeves. It ties around the waist with a sash. Both women and men in Japan wear kimonos.

Every year for the past four hundred years there has
been a kite festival in Hamamatsu, Japan. At this festival,
people fly kites that are even taller than they are!

Sayonara (sah-YOH-nah-rah)
means "good-bye" in Japanese.

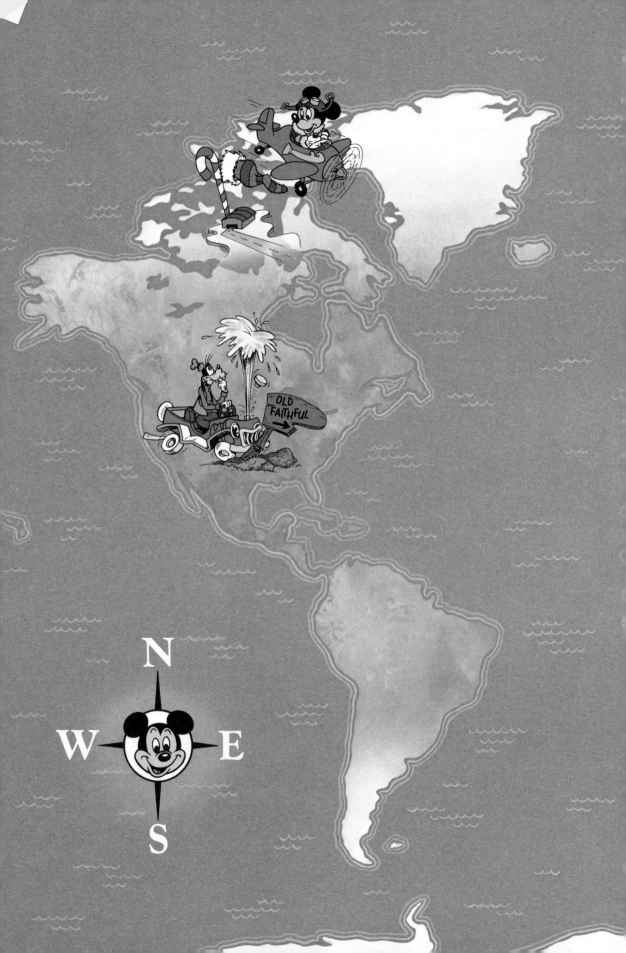